TALES
FROM THE
CRYPT®

PAPERCUTZ™

**Graphic Novels Available
from Papercutz**

Graphic Novel #1
"Ghouls Gone Wild!"

Coming December: Graphic Novel #2
"Can You Fear Me Now?"

Coming March 2008: Graphic Novel #3
"Zombielicious"

TALES FROM THE CRYPT

NO. 1 – *Ghouls Gone Wild!*

MARC BILGREY   MR. EXES
ROB VOLLMAR   TIM SMITH 3
NEIL KLEID   STEVE MANNION
DON McGREGOR   SHO MURASE
JIM SALICRUP   RICK PARKER
Writers   Artists

Based on the classic EC Comics series.

PAPERCUTZ™
New York

"BODY OF WORK!"
MARC BILGREY — Writer
MR. EXES — Artist
ORTHO THE GREAT — Letterer

"FOR SERIOUS COLLECTORS ONLY!"
ROB VOLLMAR — Writer
TIM SMITH 3 — Artist
MARK LERER — Letterer
LAURIE E. SMITH — Colorist

"THE TENANT!"
NEIL KLEID — Writer
STEVE MANNION — Artist
MARK LERER — Letterer

"RUNWAY ROADKILL!"
DON McGREGOR — Writer
SHO MURASE — Artist
with 3D CGI elements and color by **CARLOS JOSE GUZMAN**
BRYAN SENKA - Letterer

GHOULUNATIC SEQUENCES
JIM SALICRUP - Writer
RICK PARKER - Artist and Title Letterer
MARK LERER - Letterer

PREVIEW OF "THE GARDEN"
FRED VAN LENTE - Writer
MR. EXES - Artist
MARK LERER — Letterer

JIM SALICRUP
Editor-in-Chief

ISBN 10: 1-59707-082-3 paperback edition
ISBN 13: 978-1-59707-082-9 paperback edition
ISBN 10: 1-59707-083-1 hardcover edition
ISBN 13: 978-1-59707-083-6 hardcover edition

10 9 8 7 6 5 4 3 2 1

AFTER GETTING BACK TO HIS HOUSE, MIKE TOLD LINDA WHAT HAPPENED. THEN HE SHOWERED, CHANGED CLOTHES, AND TOGETHER, THEY GOT INTO THEIR CAR AND DROVE TO THEIR STORAGE UNIT OUTSIDE OF THE NEXT TOWN...

A FEW DAYS LATER, THE OWNER OF THE NEW YORK ART GALLERY CALLED THE CRANWELL POLICE TO REPORT THAT THEY HAD BEEN UNABLE TO REACH KROLL. THE POLICE CHECKED KROLL'S HOUSE AND FOUND HIS BODY...

AN INVESTIGATION FOLLOWED THAT TURNED UP NO LEADS TO THE MURDER OF JACK KROLL. BUT, BECAUSE THEY WERE HIS NEIGHBORS, MIKE AND LINDA WERE QUESTIONED...

SORRY TO BOTHER YOU FOLKS, JUST DOING MY JOB. SEE YOU AT THE POKER GAME NEXT WEEK, MIKE.

SURE, THING, CHIEF, I MEAN, MARTY.

FIVE TENANTS TESTIFY IN THE NEGLIGENCE SUIT BROUGHT AGAINST JAMES WINCHELL BY THE WILKES FAMILY.

EACH DESCRIBES THE AWFUL CONDITIONS AT 613 IGER AVENUE TO A HORRIFIED JUDGE AND JURY.

THE JUDGE, MOVED BY THE TESTIMONY AND PHOTOS OF 613 IGER, HANDS DOWN A SPECIAL SENTENCE TO JAMES WINCHELL, CHEAPSKATE LANDLORD.

WINCHELL IS ORDERED TO LIVE IN ONE OF HIS PROPERTIES FOR AN ENTIRE MONTH TO UNDERSTAND WHAT HE'S DONE TO HIS TENANTS.

EITHER HE LASTS THE MONTH IN A WINCHELL PROPERTY, WITHOUT IMPROVING ANY PART OF IT, OR THE LANDLORD LOSES EVERYTHING.

KIMBERLY KINSELLING HAS A MOMENTARY REPRIEVE FROM THE FEAR THAT SPILLS ACID INTO HER STOMACH.

SHE RELISHES THE FEAR SHE KNOWS SHE INSPIRES IN THOSE WHO WORK FOR HER. IT'S HER NAME ON THE 29TH FLOOR: KIMBERLY KINSELLING.

THAT IS HER DOMAIN. SHE IS ITS MONARCH.

SHE IS A STEELY-EYED EMPRESS WHO RULES HER DEVILISH DESIGNER DRESS DOMAIN.

SHE EXUDES HER IMPERIOUS, DEMANDING DEMEANOR—

—SO DOMINATING, SO DEVASTATING WITH WOUNDING WORDS AND WITHERING STARES—

—NONE OF HER UNDERLINGS WOULD SUSPECT THE DEMON-FEARS OF FAILURE, OF RUIN AND BANKRUPTCY, GNAWING INSIDE HER.

THERE'S THAT GAIL BROWN. SUB-
MISSIVELY STUDIOUS. PERFECT FOR
CATCHING HER PERSONAL BELONGINGS
AND MAKING SURE EVERY ITEM SHE
NEEDS IS AT THE READY.

GAIL BROWN, RIPE FOR
RIDICULE, DESPERATE
FOR PRAISE. EAGER
TO PLEASE.

GODFREY DANIELS! WHAT
IS SHE WEARING TODAY?
IT'S ONE FASHION GAFFE
AFTER ANOTHER, A STYLISH
ASSAULT ON HER SENSES
ON A DAILY BASIS.

AND THERE'S THE RELIABLE, CORTNEY, WITH HER
STARBUCKS LATTE, AND, AS USUAL, CLUTTERED DESK.

SHE HAS TO LISTEN TO THE FUMBLING EXCUSES OF THIS ASSISTANT WHO HAS NO CLUE THAT KIMBERLY KINSELLING IS ON THE LINE.

THAT SHE, KIMBERLY KINSELLING, WHO CAN SELL ANYTHING, IS IN DANGER OF LOSING HER ENTIRE WAY OF LIFE.

LOSING HER MULTI-MILLION DOLLAR APARTMENT ON PARK AVENUE IF HER LINE OF CLOTHES FAILS TONIGHT.

AND KIMBERLY KNOWS IN HER HEART, THE STYLES ARE NOT TRENDSETTERS.

SHE WILL HAVE TO SELL THEM BY THE FORCE OF HER OWN INDOMITABLE PERSONALITY.

BUT SHE KNOWS, BOTTOM LINE, SHE HERSELF WOULD SAVAGE THE NEW LINE. THE GODDESSES OF FASHION JUST WEREN'T WITH HER THIS YEAR!

I'M AFRAID I HAVE SOME BAD NEWS, MS. KINSELLING.

LIGHT FROM THE OUTSIDE WORLD FILTERS INTO KIMBERLY'S CLOISTERED INNER WORLD.

SHOWCASE LIGHTS PUNCTUATE LIKE EXCLAMATION POINTS ON COLOR AND STYLE.

KIMBERLY KINSELLING IS STRUCK ALMOST SPEECHLESS. THESE DESIGNS ARE NOT ONLY CUTTING EDGE, THEY CUT THE EYE WITH BEAUTY AND CLASS.

WITH THESE CLOTHES SHE DOESN'T HAVE TO DO A HARD SELL. WITH THESE DESIGNS, SHE'LL HAVE NO PROBLEM KEEPING HER PARK AVENUE CO-OP.

STABBING RED LIGHTS SCREAM, "COME ONE! COME ALL! SEE THE TRAGEDY!"

"IT HAPPENED TO SOMEONE ELSE, NOT YOU!"

SOME ARE WOUNDED BY WHAT THEY SEE.

TIME TO LEAVE THE SIDESHOW, GAIL!

KIMBERLY SEES ONLY SUCCESS.

WE HAVE A SHOW OF OUR OWN TO PREPARE! YOU'VE STILL GOT TONIGHT FOR ME, BEFORE YOU'RE BANISHED FOREVER! SO GET TO IT!

HAVE YOU SHOES GONE CRAZY? DO YOU KNOW WHO I AM?

KIMBERLY RUNS BLINDLY. SHE DOESN'T EVEN REALIZE IT IS THE RUNWAY WHERE SHE SOUGHT SALVATION.

THE DRESS IS TIGHTENING! SHE CAN FEEL IT SQUEEZING HER AS SURELY AND AS LETHALLY AS A PYTHON DOES ITS PREY!

SHE CAN HARDLY BREATHE. IT'S LIKE A LIVING CORSET, CRUSHING THE LIFE OUT OF HER!

THE END

THE GATE *DOESN'T CREAK* WHEN YOU OPEN IT. FOR SOME REASON THIS FACT LEAPS OUT AT YOU AS SOON AS YOU ARRIVE, DOESN'T IT, RICHARD?

THE HINGES ARE *WELL OILED*, A FRESH COAT OF PAINT *GLISTENS*, AND THERE'S NOT A SPOT OF RUST ON IT.

THE SWEETNESS OF *WILDFLOWERS* BOBBING IN THE SUN TICKLE YOUR NOSE, THE CHIRPING OF TINY *SONG-BIRDS* COMFORTS YOUR EARS.

THE TREE BOUGHS, THEY DROOP WITH *FRUIT*...

"DON'T MISS *TALES FROM THE CRYPT* NO. 2 'CAN YOU FEAR ME NOW?'"

WATCH OUT FOR PAPERCUTZ

Hi, Jim Salicrup, Editor-in-Chief of Papercutz here with the latest edition of the Papercutz Backpages.

In case you're wondering exactly what an "Editor-in-Chief of Papercutz" does, here's the answer. Papercutz, as you know, is the name of our company and we publish graphic novels for all ages, such as Nancy Drew, The Hardy Boys, Totally Spies, even The Life of Pope John Paul II… *In Comics!* These graphic novels—comics published in book form—are created by incredibly talented writers and artists, and the guy that works with them to help put it all together is the Editor-in-Chief. Sometimes, the Editor-in-Chief's job is really easy, and all he or she has to do is find great writers and artists and let them put together great comics. Other times, the Editor-in-Chief may help writers work out problems in a story, suggest to an artist how to make a page look more interesting, or just remind everyone when the art and stories are due to go off to the printer so that they can get to your favorite bookstore on time. At Papercutz, the Editor-in-Chief guy is me—Jim Salicrup.

Recently, the Museum of Comic and Cartoon Art presented an exhibit based on my career as a comicbook writer and editor, and they called it "Salicrup's Section," based on the name of my myspace blog. This is really the very first time MoCCA devoted an exhibit to someone primarily known as an editor. Usually exhibits are devoted to great comic book artists, although they recently had an exhibit devoted to Stan Lee, the co-creator of such famous characters as the Amazing Spider-Man, the Incredible Hulk, the Fantastic Four, the Uncanny X-Men, and many, many more, and even though he's one of the best comicbook editors of all time, he's primarily known as a writer. An earlier exhibit focused on Harvey Kurtzman, creator of Mad magazine. Harvey was another brilliant editor, but again, he's probably more famous for his writing and art. I can't begin to tell you how flattering it is to be honored like this, and especially when you consider whom they exhibited before. All I can say is, "I'm not worthy."

If nothing else, such a tribute has inspired me to work harder than ever to make Papercutz a great graphic novel publisher. Let me know how I'm doing by writing to me at salicrup@papercutz.com or Jim Salicrup, PAPERCUTZ, 40 Exchange Place, Ste. 1308, New York, NY 10005. For more information about the Museum of Comic and Cartoon Art go to: www.moccany.org.

Thanks,

JIM

MoCCA

Caricature of Jim drawn by Steve Brodner at the MoCCA Art Fest.

EDITOR-IN-CHIEF

PAPERCUTZ™

presents:
The Return of
TALES FROM THE CRYPT®

It's one of the biggest surprises in the world of comics and graphic novel publishing! Shortly before the 2007 New York Comic Con, Papercutz announced that we would be publishing all-new TALES FROM THE CRYPT comics. After more than 50 years, EC Comics' legendary flagship title returns with all-new shocking suspenstories, narrated by the original Crypt-Keeper, Old Witch, and Vault Keeper. Each issue will feature two 20-page tales of terror in the EC tradition! Reactions ranged from excitement—from fans thrilled to see the most famous horror comicbook ever return after over fifty years–to shock—that it was to be coming from a publisher primarily known for its Nancy Drew and The Hardy Boys graphic novels. Those books contain material suitable for all-ages, but the HBO TALES FROM THE CRYPT series certainly contained a fair amount of adult content.

"People forget that the original TALES FROM THE CRYPT comicbook, published by the legendary EC Comics back in the 50s, was also intended for all-ages, and its primary readership was young boys," Papercutz Editor-in-Chief Jim Salicrup is quick to point out. But that may be exactly what fans find so controversial. The original TALES FROM THE CRYPT comics, featured stories dreamed up by EC publisher William M. Gaines and his editor Al Feldstein, and drawn by Feldstein, as well as Graham Ingles, Jack Davis, Jack Kamen, Joe Orlando, Wally Wood, Harvey Kurtzman, Bill Elder, Reed Crandall,

Johnny Craig, Al Williamson, George Evans, and colored by Marie Severin. CRYPT started a horror comics craze that soon drew the attention of psychiatrist Dr. Frederick Wertham.

Wertham reacted to the popularity of horror comics with children by writing a book called "Seduction of the Innocent," which maintained that comics led to juvenile delinquency and even far worse behavior. Parents were understandably alarmed, and soon the Senate Subcommittee to Investigate Juvenile Delinquency was taking a hard look at comicbooks. EC Comics publisher Bill Gaines spoke before the Subcommittee, but was unable to convince them that his comics were entertaining stories told in good taste. Ultimately, comicbook publishers adversely affected by the negative publicity created the Comics Magazine Association of America which would review comics and award a seal of approval to assure parents that the comic's contents were safe, wholesome entertainment. Unfortunately, it was too late for many publishers, who went bankrupt as the negative publicity had hurt sales of comics terribly. EC Comics, tried to hang in there, but despite canceling their horror comics, and creating new titles such as "Valor" and "Psychoanalysis," only MAD comics, in a new magazine format, survived.

The question is, was TALES FROM CRYPT really all that bad? "Of course not!" Salicrup insists. "Ironically, many of the original stories would be approved by today's revised Comics Code. But sure, there were some stories that still wouldn't get by. The point here is that the stories that Papercutz will be creating will be aimed at readers age 10 and up. Instead of excessive blood and gore, we'll be sticking to the TALES FROM THE CRYPT tradition of stories filled with interesting characters, lots of dark humor, and of course, the trademarked EC "shock" endings!" The first TALES FROM THE CRYPT comic from Papercutz, which will be on sale in comics shops in June, features:

• "Body of Work," by horror author Marc Bilgrey (H.P. Lovecraft's Magazine of Horror, "And Don't Forget to Rescue the Princess") and Mr. Exes (Abra Cadaver). The story reveals how two nosy and somewhat murderous neighbors discover the shocking inspiration for Jack Kroll's creepy "outsider" artwork.

• "For Serious Collectors Only," by Rob Vollmar (Bluesman) and Tim Smith III (Teen Titans Go!). This tale explores how far Thomas Donalley— a middle-aged action-figure collector who lives in his Mom's basement— will go for an ultra-rare Japanese figure.

• Introductory pages featuring the GhouLunatics are written by editor Jim Salicrup and drawn by artist Rick Parker (Beavis and Butt-Head).

• Cover by award-winning artist Kyle Baker (Nat Turner, Plastic Man, Why I Hate Saturn). Future issues will include stories by Fred Van Lente (Marvel Adventures), Xeric Grant winner Neil Kleid, Stefan Petrucha (The Shadow of Frankenstein, NANCY DREW), Don McGregor (ZORRO), Sho Murase (NANCY DREW), and other great talents. Each bi-monthly issue is 48 full-color pages for an affordable $3.95. Naturally, the comics will be collected in the usual 112 page, ($7.95 paperback; $12.95 hardcover) full-color digest format with more previously unseen stories, the first volume, TALES FROM THE CRYPT *"Ghouls Gone Wild!"* available in bookstores everywhere in time for Halloween.

When reached for comment, the Crypt-Keeper said, "It's good to be back, boils and ghouls—and it's about time! Ahahahah!"

Recently on papercutz.com we featured a special Match Wits with the Hardy Boys promotion. (See, why it's important to drop by our website whenever you can? You never know what surprises you may discover!) Well, the Hardy Boys promotion is officially over, and now...

Papercutz is proud to announce the GRAND PRIZE WINNER of the MATCH WITS WITH THE HARDY BOYS—

JEREMY HAFTEL!

CONGRATULATIONS, JEREMY!

Jeremy's entry was one of several that correctly found the clues requested. Here are the original questions along with Jeremy's answers:

On page twenty-nine, can you find the clue that indicates that there are Hardy Boys imposters aboard this souped-up bullet train? Here's a hint: This is the kind of pointed clue that could only appear in a comicbook or graphic novel. This may be just a simple case of seeing is believing!

Jeremy's answer:
Looking into the window from outside of the train, you see two people who look like the Hardy Boys. They are not talking. The dialogue balloons are coming from other windows where you cannot see the Hardy Boys from the outside. So, it appears that the ones that you can see from outside are imposters.

Page thirty has a major clue that something funny is going on aboard this trouble-train! What is it? Here's a hint: If you booked passage on this debut run of this super-duper bullet train, what would you find suspicious by its absence?

Jeremy's answer:
If this is the debut run, you would expect the dining car to be crowded with people and at least some food being served. There is no food, no water and no food servers (and very few people).

Here's something you don't see on trains, even super-luxury trains like this one. What telltale clue are the boys overlooking on page thirty-three? Here's a hint: If you ever bunked with a buddy on a train, or even seen a sleeping car on TV or in a movie, you'll spot what's wrong here—unless we caught you napping!

Jeremy's answer:
The word "bunked" makes you believe that the bed should be bunk beds. These beds are not bunk beds and the one on the left looks like it is not supported by anything other than the wall and the other bed which is barely touching it and would not make sense.

Great job, Jeremy! For your efforts you will be rewarded with a guest-starring role as an agent of A.T.A.C. in an upcoming Hardy Boys graphic novel. You'll be helping Frank and Joe make the world a much safer place. Be sure to keep an eye on all announcements at www.papercutz.com for the title and publication date.

Although, Jeremy is our big winner, everyone at Papercutz extends a big THANK-YOU to all of our cunning clue-seekers! We were all knocked out by the incredible response and impressed by the high degree of sleuthing skills evident in each of the entries! Thanks, everyone, for making the Match Wits With The Hardy Boys promotion such a success!

THE HARDY BOYS IN OTHER MEDIA!

While everyone is excited and thrilled by the all-new Nancy Drew movie, starring Emma Roberts, here's an announcement we're sure all Papercutz fans will be equally thrilled and excited by...

Filming may begin in 2008 on THE HARDY MEN, starring Tom Cruise and Ben Stiller!!

According to The Hollywood Reporter, "Mr. And Mrs. Smith" screenwriter Simon Kinberg is currently working on the script for the big-screen comedy, which follows the grown up adventures of Frank and Joe Hardy. Shawn Levy is set to be the film's director.

But let's face it, the movie's still a long time away, probably 2009 at the earliest. Lucky for us there are plenty of Hardy Boys books and graphic novels to enjoy in the meantime. But this also gives us an excuse to celebrate earlier incarnations of the Hardy Boys in other media with the following playlists and episode guides to the vinyl records and animated series.

In September 1969 The Hardy Boys debuted on the ABC television network in an animated series produced by Filmation Studios. To make the show similar to the then-hit animated Archies animated series, Frank and Joe not only solved mysteries, they had a rock band as well!

Here's an episode guide to the animated Hardy Boys TV series produced by Filmation Studios. All episodes were aired on the ABC Network in color and were 30 minutes each, with two mystery stories. The second season was all reruns of the first season's episodes. They were all directed by Hal Sutherland and produced by Lou Scheimer and Norm Prescott. Trying to faithfully adapt an entire Hardy Boys novel into a cartoon that's less than fifteen minutes long would be impossible, so the show's writers loosely adapted original Franklin W. Dixon stories, using story elements from the original series as inspiration.

Episode One: (Titles unknown) aired September 6, 1969.

Episode Two: "The Secret Warning" and "The Viking Symbol Mystery" aired September 13, 1969.

Episode Three: "The Secret of the Caves" and "The Secret of the Old Mill" aired September 20, 1969.

Episode Four: "The Missing Chums" and "The Mystery of the Desert Giants" aired September 27, 1969.

Episode Five: "The Mystery of Cabin Island" and "Hunting for Hidden Gold" aired October 4, 1969.

Episode Six: "The Mystery of the Aztec Warrior" and "The Hidden Harbor Mystery" aired October 11, 1969.

Episode Seven: "The Ghost At Skeleton Rock" and "Mystery of the Chinese Junk" aired October 18, 1969.

Episode Eight: "The Shore Road Mystery" and "What Happened At Midnight" aired October 25, 1969.

Episode Nine: "The Sign of the Crooked Arrow" and "The Clue in the Embers" aired November 1, 1969.

Episode Ten: "The Clue of the Screeching Owl" and "The House on the Cliff" aired November 8, 1969.

Episode Eleven: "Mystery of the Spiral Bridge" and "The Yellow Feather Mystery" aired November 15, 1969.

Episode Twelve: "The Mystery of Devil's Paw" and "The Sinister Sign Post" aired November 22, 1969.

Episode Thirteen: "The Melted Coins" and "The Mark on the Door" aired November 29, 1969.

Episode Fourteen: "The Flickering Torch Mystery" and "The Haunted Fort" aired December 6, 1969.

Episode Fifteen: "The Mystery of Wildcat Swamp" and "The Clue of the Broken Blade" aired December 13, 1969.

Episode Sixteen: (Title unknown) and "The Short Wave Mystery" and aired December 20, 1969.

Episode Seventeen: "The Hooded Hawk Mystery" and "The Secret of Pirate's Hill" aired December 27, 1969.

A group of musicians were recruited by Bill Traut and Jim Golden of Dunwich Productions, Chicago with the help of the show's producers, Filmation, to record for RCA and go out on the road to perform the songs live. So Frank Hardy was played by Reed Kailing, of The Destinations—a band that played at the wedding of President Johnson's daughter, Lucy. Jeff Taylor was hired to be Joe Hardy. Deven English was Wanda Kay Breckenridge, a character created for the cartoons. Norbet (Nibs) Soltysiak became Chubby Morton, a character obviously based on Chet Morton. And drummer Bob Crowder, who had played with the Shirelles and others, was Pete Jones, a character created for the cartoons, who was the first regular African-American character on an animated TV series. The musical Hardy Boys band appeared live at the end of the animated episodes, and on the covers of the four Gold Key Hardy Boys comicbooks based on the cartoons.

Two albums were released by The Hardy Boys, "Here Come The Hardy Boys" and "Wheels." Here are the album covers and the song lists:

Here Come the Hardys
(Theme from cartoon TV series)
Those Country Girls
One Time in a Million
That's That
(I Want You to) Be My Baby
Sink or Swim
Namby-Pamby
My Little Sweet Pea
Sha-La-La
Fees So Good
Love and Let Love
Wheels
Old Man Moses Front Porch Rhythm Band
Carnival Time
Good Good Lovin'
Let the Sun Shine Down
Long, Long Way to Nashville
Love Train
Archie Brown
Where Would I Be
I Hear the Grass Singin'
Baby, This is the Last Time

That last song sure was prophetic, as it truly was the last Hardy Boys song from this groovy band! But who knows? Maybe one of these songs may turn up on the soundtrack to the Hardy Men movie? Stranger things have happened!

PAPERCUT Z ™
Feedback

We've been asking for feedback, and we've been getting it! For example...

Dear Mr. Salicrup,

I just finished reading Nancy Drew graphic novel #7 "The Charmed Bracelet" and saw your article at the end of the book saying you want to hear from your readers.

My name is Nancy, I am 31 years old and I am absolutely crazy about these new ND graphic novels! The first one I read was "Haunted Dollhouse." I really enjoyed the storyline and the references to the original ND series. I also think the artistry is fantastic. I had never even looked at a graphic novel before and only looked into these because they are Nancy Drew. I've been buying the whole series as they come out and I hope they will be around for a while.

I do have a question for you... I just picked up a copy of "Global Warning." I started reading it and realized that the pictures on page 3 are the same as on page 7. The writing makes sense on page 7, but not page 3. Was this a printing error? Just curious...

I look forward to hearing from you...

Sincerely,
Nancy M. DeVault

You're right, Nancy—there was a mistake and that wasn't the correct page. We're presenting the correct page 3 on the very next page.

We hope our Nancy Drew graphic novels will be around as long as Nancy Drew is around. With the new Nancy Drew movie creating a whole new generation of Nancy Drew fans, and considering that Nancy Drew has already been around for over 75 years, all that makes us very optimistic about the future.

We also heard from hundreds of other Papercutz fans. Seems that they're thrilled with the stories, characters, and artwork in all our graphic novels, and the only complaint some have is that we don't come out with more books—that it's tough waiting three months for the next book in a Papercutz graphic novel series. Well, we understand and we'd love to come out with a new book every month, but our artists and writers can only draw and write so fast! There's just no way we can produce our titles any faster and still maintain the excellent level of writing and artwork that you're telling us you love so much.

But hey! We're happy to report that Papercutz graphic novels are also available at many Public Libraries, and we couldn't be happier. As proud as we are of Nancy Drew, Totally Spies, Zorro, The Hardy Boys, and all the rest, we certainly don't want anyone to miss a meal or go broke buying Papercutz graphic novels. So, visit your local Public Library and check us out.

And speaking of libraries, fans want to know where they can buy hardcover editions of Papercutz graphic novels, just like the ones in the libraries. The answer is, you can buy them from your favorite bookstore or direct from Papercutz (see our ads elsewhere in this book). If your bookstore doesn't have any in stock, we're sure they'll be happy to order the books for you. Or check the major online booksellers—they all have the hardcover editions available. We have to admit, we're fans of our hardcover editions just because we love how they look on our bookshelves.

We're just about out of room, but we want you to keep those emails and letters coming! Write to: salicrup@papercutz.com or Jim Salicrup, Papercutz, 40 Exchange Place, Ste. 1308, New York, NY 10005. Thanks for all the feedback—we really appreciate it!